Ladybird I'm Ready... for Phonics!

Note to parents, carers and teachers

Ladybird I'm Ready for Phonics is a series of phonic reading books that have been carefully written to give gradual, structured practice of the synthetic phonics programme your child is learning at school.

Each book focuses on a set of phonemes (sounds) together with their graphemes (letters). The books also provide practice of common tricky words, such as **the** and **said**, that cannot be sounded out.

The series closely follows the order that your child is taught phonics in school, from initial letter sounds to key phonemes and beyond. It helps to build reading confidence through practice of these phonics building blocks, and reinforces school learning in a fun way.

Ideas for use

- Children learn best when reading is a fun experience. Read the book together and give your child plenty of praise and encouragement.

- Help your child identify and sound out the phonemes (sounds) in any words he is having difficulty reading. Then, blend these sounds together to read the word.

- Talk about the story words and tricky words at the end of the stories to reinforce learning.

For more information and advice on synthetic phonics and school book banding, visit **www.ladybird.com/phonics**

Book Band 4

Level 10 reinforces the phonics learnt in levels 1 to 9, as children practise longer words.

Special features:

repetition of sounds in different words

short sentences with simple language

Some children were running near the river. One of them fell in.

Help! Help! I can not swim!

6

7

Story Words

Can you match these words to the pictures below?

children

river

ring

dog

shook

black

brown

16

Tricky Words

These tricky words are in the story you have just read. They cannot be phonetically sounded out. Can you memorize them and read them super fast?

some   out

were   what

one   when

do

there

17

summary page to reinforce learning

Written by Monica Hughes
Illustrated by Ian Cunliffe

Phonics and Book Banding Consultant: Kate Ruttle

A catalogue record for this book is available from the British Library

Published by Ladybird Books Ltd
80 Strand, London, WC2R 0RL
A Penguin Company

001

ISBN: 978-0-72327-546-6
Printed in China

Ladybird I'm Ready...
for Phonics!

The River Dog

Some children were running near the river. One of them fell in.

There was a ring on the
river bank. A big lad grabbed it
and tossed it into the river.

The ring floated in the river, but it was too far for Janet to get it.

Just then, a big black and brown dog ran up. It was Wowzer!

The children were afraid of the dog, but they did not need to be. Wowzer was a clever dog. He did not bark or growl.

Wowzer did not wait. He jumped into the river.

He swam to the ring and tugged it across to Janet.

Janet held on to the ring.
Now she was well!
Wowzer tugged the ring and Janet
back to the river bank.

The children helped Janet out
of the river. What do you think
Wowzer did when he got out?

He just shook himself
and then ran off.

Story Words

Can you match these words
to the pictures below?

children

river

ring

dog

shook

black

brown

Tricky Words

These tricky words are in the story you have just read. They cannot be phonetically sounded out. Can you memorize them and read them super fast?

some

out

were

what

one

when

do

there

Ladybird I'm Ready... for Phonics!

A Winter Storm

It was winter. The road had drifts on it when Cliff and Stella were off to visit Gran.

All of a sudden there was a storm.

The little children started to run. Cliff fell down and hurt one of his legs.

"I can not stand," moaned Cliff. "You must go and get help."

The wind got stronger and the drifts got deeper. Soon, Cliff vanished under a deep drift.

Help! Help!

Then Wowzer, the black and brown
dog, was there. He dug and dug.
At last, he had dug a tunnel
into the drift.

Wowzer kept digging until he got to Cliff. He grabbed Cliff's jacket and tugged. He tugged Cliff right out of the tunnel.

Just as they were at the end of the
tunnel, Stella got back with help.

What do you think Wowzer
did then?

Well, he was shivering so he shook himself and just ran off.

Story Words

Can you match these words
to the pictures below?

leg

Cliff

Stella

Wowzer

jacket

Tricky Words

These tricky words are in the story you have just read. They cannot be phonetically sounded out. Can you memorize them and read them super fast?

do	out
when	what
were	so
there	one
little	

Collect all
Ladybird I'm Ready...
for Phonics!

Captain Comet's Space Party

9780723275374

Nat Naps!

9780723275381

Top Dog

9780723275398

Huff! Puff! Run!

9780723275404

Fix It Vets

9780723275411

Dash is Fab!

9780723275428

Big, Big Fish

9780723275435

Dig, Farmer, Dig!

9780723275442

Fun Fair Fun

9780723275459

Wow, Wowzer!

9780723275466

Wizard Woody

9780723275473

Monster Stars

9780723275480

Say the Sounds

9780723271598

Flashcards

9780723272069

Ladybird I'm Ready for... apps are now available for iPad, iPhone and iPod touch.

Apps also available on Android devices